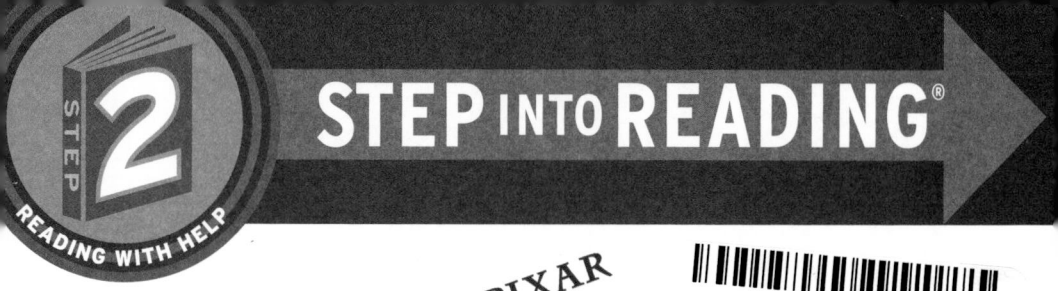

W9-CBZ-889

Disney · PIXAR
INSIDE OUT

MOM, DAD, AND ME

by Christy Webster

Random House New York

This is Riley.
She lives with
her mom and dad
in a small town.

Mom and Dad take good care of Riley. They all love each other very much.

Mom is smart and kind.

She gives the best hugs!

Dad is silly and fun.

He likes to play games.

Mom, Dad, and Riley
love their home.
There is a lake
near their house.

It is the perfect place
for Riley to grow up!

Riley, Mom, and Dad
love to play hockey.

Hooray!

Riley scores a goal!

Riley has made
lots of memories
over the years.
Some are happy.

Some are sad.

Some are both!

One day,

Dad gets a new job

in a big city.

They sell their house

and move away.

Moving is hard
for Riley.
It is sad to leave
her old life behind.

The new house
is nothing
like the old one.
It does not feel
like home.

Riley goes
to a new school.
Will she make
new friends?

Mom has an idea.
She helps Riley join
a new hockey team!

Riley likes being
part of the team.
After a while,
she makes lots
of new friends.

Mom and Dad are
still her biggest fans.

Riley learns that
some things change.

But Mom and Dad will always be there for her.

Family is forever.